Dedicated to my favorite rhyming monsters, Calvin and Lucy. — LF

Dedicated to my parents and my Toffee. —PJ

For permission requests by smart goblins and witty witches, write to the publisher at www.lisaferland.com

ISBN 978-0-9970624-8-9

When The Clock Strikes On Halloween

Written By Lisa Ferland

Illustrated By Pei Jen

When the clock strikes one...

Mummies come undone.

When the clock strikes two...

Witches stir their brew.

When the clock strikes three,

Goblins need to pee.

When the clock strikes four...

Zombies break the door.

When the clock strikes five,

Shadows come alive,

When the clock strikes six...

Witches fly on sticks.

When the clock strikes seven...

You meet a ghost named Kevin.

When the clock strikes eight...

Vampires crash the gate.

When the clock strikes nine...

Jack-O'-Lanterns shine.

When the clock strikes ten...

Werewolves leave their den.

When the clock strikes eleven...

Yippee! Candy heaven!

When the clock strikes twelve,
it's midnight...

Everything is going to be all right.
Just some kids out for a fright.

Halloween was full of
tricks and fun.

Good night, good night, spooky one.

Discussion Questions

1. At three o'clock, the goblins need to pee.
What should they do instead of standing in the woods?

    A. Hold it and say nothing
    B. Do a little dance
    C. Tell an adult and find a bathroom

2. When the clock strikes seven and you meet a ghost named Kevin, is that in the afternoon or evening?

3. How many hours passed during the entire story for the characters?

4. There is a little clue on every page that each monster is really a neighborhood kid. Can you find each clue?

5. Which illustration is your favorite and why?

6. Can you write new rhymes for each hour? What happens when the clock strikes at your house?

ABOUT THE AUTHOR

Lisa Ferland is a writer and mother to a ninja warrior and a dancing firefly. She and her family live in Sweden but she's called many places home. Connect with Lisa at lisaferland.com.

ABOUT THE ILLUSTRATOR

Pei Jen is a Malaysian illustrator who loves bringing magic into children's books. She has loved drawing since she was a kid and experiments learning new artistic styles in both fantasy and realism. You can follow her work on Instagram at @toffeefingerart.

If you enjoyed the book, please leave a review on Amazon or Goodreads!

Show us your books!

Tag us on social media with
#whentheclockstrikes

Instagram: @lisaferland_
Facebook: lisaferlandconsulting

Subscribe to be notified when the next book is ready:
www.lisaferland.com/when-the-clock-strikes-series

Be sure to read the next book in the series for more fun every hour!

Made in the USA
Las Vegas, NV
23 September 2021